LBP

THIS BOOK BELONGS TO

_____

TM

THE LIMA BEAR STORIES

THE LABYRINTH

STORY BY

Thomas Weck *and* Peter Weck

ILLUSTRATIONS BY

Len DiSalvo

LIMA BEAR PRESS, LLC
Wilmington, Delaware

Published by Lima Bear Press, LLC

Lima Bear Press, LLC
2305 MacDonough Rd., Suite 201
Wilmington, DE 19805-2620
FOR VOLUME SALES: sales@limabearpress.com

Visit us on the web at
www.limabearpress.com

Book & Cover design by: rosa+wesley, inc.

Printed in the United States of America

FIRST EDITION
ISBN: 978-1-933872-04-9

Weck, Thomas L., 1942-
    The Labyrinth / story by Thomas Weck and Peter Weck; illustrations by Len DiSalvo. — 1st ed.

    p. : col. ill. ; cm. — (The Lima Bear stories)

    Summary: The Duke, Mean Ol' Bean, is unhappy when Princess Belinda Bean takes the throne as
Queen and Ruler of Beandom. The Duke lures the Princess into a magic labyrinth from which there
is no escape. When L. Joe Bean discovers the plot, his cleverness wins the day.
    Interest age group: 004-008.
    ISBN: 978-1-933872-04-9

    1. Bears—Juvenile fiction. 2. Queens—Juvenile fiction. 3. Labyrinths—Juvenile fiction.
4. Wisdom—Juvenile fiction. 5. Bears—Fiction. 6. Kings, queens, rulers, etc.—Fiction.
7. Labyrinths—Fiction. 8. Wisdom—Fiction.
I. Weck, Peter (Peter M.) II. DiSalvo, Len. III. Title.

PZ7.W432 Lab 2012
[Fic]

Our kind and good King Limalot Bear,
Ruled over his land so very fair.

His heart still glowed a gentle green,
But he'd grown too old for the royal scene.

There was no prince. No son he had,
But a lovely princess called him "Dad".

Said he, "Dear Princess Belinda Bean
O'er all my lands I'll make you queen."

Alas, within the Beandom's walls
    Another heard his kingship's calls.

"I will be king," said Mean ol' Bean.
    "You wait and see," said this furry fiend.

Oh dear! Oh my! What will be seen!
    What might he do to Princess Bean?

And who will protect Belinda Bean
    So she can stay the rightful queen?

Queen Belinda Bean sat on her throne for the first time. Everyone cheered—everyone, that is, except for Mean ol' Bean. He wanted to be the king instead.

OH, MEAN OL' BEAN
    HOW HE DID SCHEME.
TO BE RID OF THE QUEEN,
    THAT WAS HIS DREAM.

One who cheered was L. Joe Bean, the wisest man in Beandom. Like his cousin, Lima Bear, he came from a special clan of beans— all very small. In fact, L. Joe Bean looked like a pinto bean.

Now, in beautiful Beandom, near Queen Belinda's castle, there was a **huge** labyrinth. It was said that there was a magic flower garden at its center. But no one had ever seen it. The labyrinth had so many *twists* and *turns* that even if you found your way into the magic garden, you might never find your way out.

OH, MEAN OL' BEAN
HOW HE DID SCHEME.
TO BE RID OF THE QUEEN,
THAT WAS HIS DREAM.

Mean ol' Bean knew how much
Queen Belinda loved flowers. "Aha!" he
said. "I have a plan. I'll find the magic
garden. Then I'll lead the queen there
and trap her in the labyrinth forever."

Every day, secretly (or so he thought), Mean ol' Bean rode into the labyrinth in his black chariot. He followed many different *twists* and *turns* trying to find the magic garden. Each time, Mean ol' Bean was careful to leave behind a trail of pink flower petals so he could find his way out. What he did not know was that L. Joe Bean was watching him.

OH, MEAN OL' BEAN
HOW HE DID SCHEME.
TO BE RID OF THE QUEEN,
THAT WAS HIS DREAM.

Finally, after many days of searching, Mean ol' Bean found the magic garden! The flowers were all the colors of the rainbow, and they glowed as bright as the sun.

The very next day Mean ol' Bean told Queen Belinda he would lead her to the magic garden.

Mean ol' Bean's black chariot led the way. Queen Belinda followed in her golden chariot. Secretly, L. Joe Bean followed them in his tiny chariot—a small, pearly seashell on wheels, pulled by nine bees.

OH, MEAN OL' BEAN
  HOW HE DID SCHEME.
TO BE RID OF THE QUEEN,
  THAT WAS HIS DREAM.

As Queen Belinda's chariot carried her into the magic garden, she was dazzled by the rainbow of flowers.

OH, MEAN OL' BEAN
    HOW HE DID SCHEME.
TO BE RID OF THE QUEEN,
    THAT WAS HIS DREAM.

It was just as Mean ol' Bean had planned. All he had to do was follow his path of pink petals out of the labyrinth, leaving Queen Belinda trapped inside the maze. But, as Mean ol' Bean turned to flee, a sudden gust of wind blew all the pink petals high into the air, scattering them in all directions!

"No!" Mean ol' Bean shouted. Then he gripped his reins tightly and mumbled to himself, "I…I know the way out. I've done it before." He raced away willy-nilly, almost knocking over L. Joe Bean's chariot. What was *he* doing here?

L. Joe Bean figured out Mean ol' Bean's evil scheme. He shouted for Queen Belinda to quickly follow Mean ol' Bean's chariot. But her chariot was not *fast* enough. But it didn't matter. Mean ol' Bean was lost in the labyrinth. He turned this way and that but he could NOT find his way out.

They all got so mixed up! At one point, Queen Belinda and L. Joe Bean saw Mean ol' Bean's chariot heading straight for them. Mean ol' Bean tried to grab L. Joe Bean, but he missed. L. Joe Bean reached up with his tiny sword and, with two quick slashes, cut a large L on the side of the black chariot. That made Mean ol' Bean very angry.

Suddenly, L. Joe Bean had an idea. He climbed onto the back of one of his bees and flew above the top of the nearest wall of the labyrinth. From this spot, L. Joe Bean saw the way out of the labyrinth.

"Quick, Your Majesty, follow me," he called out.

Mean ol' Bean heard L. Joe Bean's shout. All he had to do was follow the golden chariot and he, too, would find the way out.

"Not so fast," thought L. Joe Bean. He stopped in mid-air, turned, and flew back. His bee swooped down and stung Mean ol' Bean right on the end of his nose.

"Ow! Ow! OW!" Mean ol' Bean howled in pain! His nose grew big and red. But he held on tight and stayed on his black chariot.

L. Joe Bean's bee dove down and stung him again. Mean ol' Bean's nose swelled bigger and redder, but still he stayed on his chariot. Down again swooped L. Joe Bean on his bee. ZAP!!! Right on the very tip of his nose again! This time Mean ol' Bean fell off the black chariot. His nose hurt so much he could not get up.

L. Joe Bean swept down one more time and slashed a large L into the heavy cloth of Mean ol' Bean's coat. Then he flew back to his chariot and led the queen to safety.

21

Queen Belinda was grateful to L. Joe Bean. She had a Royal Sword made to fit L. Joe Bean's hand. The sword glistened with gold and the handle was covered with precious jewels. Then, with two lightning-quick swishes of the golden sword, he carved a beautiful L in the ground near the queen's feet.

Everyone cheered, "Hooray! Hooray!"

23

As for Mean ol' Bean, the other beans heard him rushing back and forth trying to find his way out of the labyrinth. He had been trapped by his own evil plan. Finally, L. Joe Bean took pity on him. He hopped on one of his trusty bees, and flew back to Mean ol' Bean.

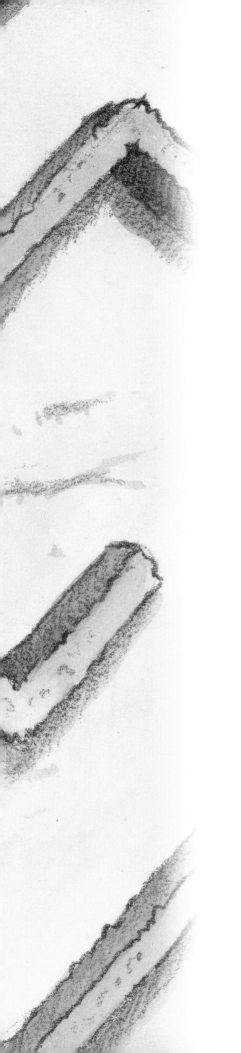

When he saw L. Joe Bean on his bee, Mean ol' Bean hid his head, afraid that he was going to be stung again. But L. Joe Bean got off his bee and started to speak.

"Mean ol' Bean, I do not want you to be trapped here forever. If you promise to leave the Kingdom of Beandom, I will lead you out of the labyrinth."

"I do promise! I do!" Mean ol' Bean said as fast as he could.

After Mean ol' Bean had gone, L. Joe Bean had one more idea. He made a pathway of tiny bricks leading into the labyrinth. It led right to the magic garden, so all the beans in Beandom could enjoy the beauty of the flowers and still find their way safely home every time.

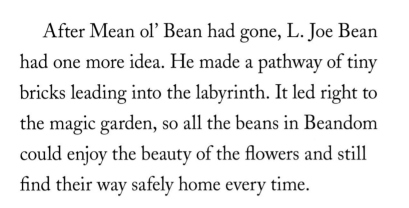

THE END

EXTEND THE LEARNING

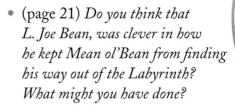

Read *The Labyrinth.*

Before reading, you might ask:

- Build background knowledge about labyrinths. Let children know a labyrinth is a place full of passageways or paths designed to make it difficult to find your way around. A labyrinth is similar to a maze.
- Discuss what children know about mazes. Have them share personal experiences, such as completing a paper maze or walking through a corn maze. Guide them to share specific details. *What types of mazes do you like to solve? What makes a maze challenging? Have you ever walked through a maze? What did it look like?*
- Read the title and briefly discuss details in the cover illustration. Browse through the first few pages. Help children set a purpose for reading, such as *I want to find out what happens in the labyrinth.*
- *Let's read* The Labyrinth *to find out if L. Joe Bean is able to figure out Mean ol' Bean's scheme to get rid of Queen Belinda Bean.*

During reading, stop and ask children questions to make sure they are following along. Take time to talk about details in the illustrations to help children understand story concepts and unfamiliar vocabulary. Ask questions such as:

- (page 8) *How does the illustration help you understand that Mean ol' Bean is evil?*
- (page 14) *What happens after the big gust of wind? How does this impact the story's plot?*
- (page 19) *How does L. Joe Bean help the queen out of the labyrinth?*

- (page 21) *Do you think that L. Joe Bean, was clever in how he kept Mean ol'Bean from finding his way out of the Labyrinth? What might you have done?*
- (page 21) *Can you fill in the missing word?* L. Joe Bean swept down one more time and _____ his initial "L" on the front of Mean ol' Bean's jacket.

After reading, take time to talk about the book. You might ask:

- *Tell me what this story is mostly about.*
- *What parts of the story did you find interesting?*
- *What words would you use to describe Mean ol' Bean? What do you think motivates him?*
- *Tell me three things in your home that glisten like a gold sword.*
- *Let's look for details in the story that help you visualize the labyrinth.*
- *Would you follow Mean ol' Bean into the labyrinth? Why or why not?*
- *How would you feel if you got lost in the labyrinth? What would you do to make sure you could find your way out?*
- *Mean ol'Bean, Queen Belinda, and L. Joe Bean rode into the labyrinth on their chariots. Can you recall details about each of the chariots?*
  Mean ol' Bean: a black chariot pulled by a gator
  Queen Belinda: a gold chariot pulled by two ladybugs
  L. Joe Bean: a small pearl seashell chariot pulled by nine bees
- Reread the story together as a choral reading. Have one person read the narrative text while the other joins in with the rhyming refrain.

ACTIVITIES!

- **Wind Watcher**   Some winds are gentle. Other winds can be gusty enough to make trees sway and flags flap. Keep a notebook to record the wind in your area for a week or two. Date your notebook. Record your observations. Keep an eye out for clues that show how fast the wind is blowing. Do you notice trees swaying? Are leaves rustling? Are flags flapping in the wind? Use the Beaufort scale below to record how fast the wind is blowing. Check the weather section in your newspaper for current information about wind speeds.

Beaufort #	Description	Things to See on Land
0	Calm	Smoke rises straight up
1	Light air	Smoke drifts in the wind direction; weather vanes do not move
2	Light breeze	Leaves and weather vanes move; light breeze felt on face
3	Gentle breeze	Leaves and twigs moving constantly
4	Moderate breeze	Leaves and loose paper rise up; small branches move; flags flap
5	Fresh breeze	Small trees begin to sway
6	Strong breeze	Large branches sway
7	Strong wind	Larger trees sway; flags stand straight out; resistance felt when walking against the wind

- **Design a sidewalk maze**   Share examples of simple mazes made with circle, octagon, or star shapes. Draw children's attention to the point to enter the maze and the path to the center of each shape. Then use chalk to make a gigantic shape on a sidewalk or on the blacktop at a playground. Begin at the center of the shape to make a path that leads to the outside wall of your shape. Then add paths inside the shape that twist and turn. Make sure your paths are wide enough for people to walk through. Draw an arrow to show where to enter your maze. Think of something clever to put in the center, such as a colorful magic garden.

- **Shades of Meaning**   Mean ol' Bean mumbled to himself when he was trying to find his way out of the labyrinth. Draw attention to the word *mumble*. Ask what *mumble* means in this context (to speak quietly and unclearly). Talk about words with similar meanings, such as *whisper*, *murmur*, *babble*, and *mutter*. Plan time for children to act out the meanings of each of these words. Help them notice the subtle differences between them.

- **Word Sort**   Let children know that some consonants make two different sounds. Direct them to listen to the sound the letter g makes in *magic* and *garden*. Write *magic* and *garden* on index cards. Then work with children to locate the following words in the story: *gentle* (page 1), *huge* (page 4), *golden* (page 10), *gust* (page 14), *guessed* (page 16), *big* (page 20), *gold* (page 23), and *gone* (page 26). Write each word on an index card. Invite them to add one or more words that, like the key words, have a 'g' sound: (magic) *gem*, *gym* and *germ*; (garden) *got*, *golf*, and *gave*.

Tell children to listen to the sound the letter g makes in each word. Slowly say each word aloud as you sort the words into the two categories. Ask volunteers to tell if the word goes with *magic* or *garden*. When all the words are sorted, read the list of word cards aloud.

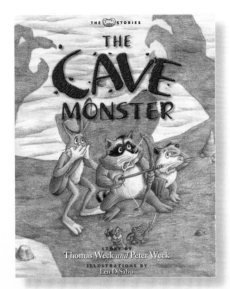

Oh, no!!! L. Joe Bean, Lima Bear's cousin, has been captured by the Cave Monster. Lima Bear and his friends enter the dangerous Black Cave to save L. Joe Bean. The Cave Monster attacks. Will they save L. Joe Bean in time? And will they save themselves? Read on to see how bravely they fight the Cave Monster.

THE MESSAGE OF THE STORY IS:
Friends, individually afraid, find courage when acting together.

$15.95

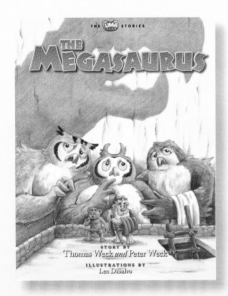

What's the King of Beandom to do? The tiny, multi-colored beans of Beandom are under attack by a monster. Even the King's wisest advisors seem unable to find a solution. Who will save Beandom? Can an ordinary tiny bean step forward with a plan that works?

Welcome to Beandom! It's a great place to visit. Or, it will be—just as soon as we get rid of that pesky monster!

THE MESSAGE OF THE STORY IS:
Follow your convictions even when others think differently.

$15.95

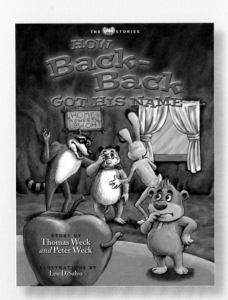

Can you imagine what it would be like to lose your back!!? Well, that is exactly what happens to Plumpton, the Opossum. Lima Bear and his clever friends become detectives searching for his missing back. Follow them as they try new and different ways of thinking to solve the mystery. See how they band together to protect each other in times of danger! Will they ever find Plumpton's back? Follow the story to find the answer.

THE MESSAGE OF THE STORY IS:
The tolerance of differences in others yields benefits.

$15.95